Cycling Science

James Bow

Crabtree Publishing Company

Crabtree Publishing Company

www.crabtreebooks.com

Author: James Bow

Editors: Molly Aloian
Leon Gray

Proofreaders: Katherine Berti
Reagan Miller
Adrianna Morganelli
Crystal Sikkens

Project coordinator: Robert Walker

Production coordinator: Margaret Amy Salter

Prepress technician: Margaret Amy Salter

Designer: Lynne Lennon

Picture researcher: Sean Hannaway

Managing editor: Tim Cooke

Art director: Jeni Child

Design manager: David Poole

Editorial director: Lindsey Lowe

Children's publisher: Anne O'Daly

Photographs:
Action Plus: page 14
Alamy: D. Hurst: page 9 (bottom); Greenwales: page 11 (top);
    Ian Nolan: page 12; Seb Rogers: pages 20, 25 (top), 26–27;
    Tristan Hawke: page 25 (bottom)
Corbis: Tim de Waele: pages 4–5, 23; Elizabeth Kreutz: page
    11 (bottom); Bettmann: page 13 (top); Josef Scaylea: page
    13 (center); Mike King: page 15 (bottom)
Getty Images: Franck Fife: page 8; Jamie Squire: page 22
Harald Cramer: pages 28–29
John Cassidy: page 29
PA Photos: Simon Grimmett: page 5 (bottom); Boris Roessler:
    page 9 (top)
Photolibrary Group: Dennis Kunkel: page 7 (top)
Public Domain: page 17 (bottom right)
Rex Features: Action Press: page 7 (bottom)
Science Photo Library: Laurent BSIP: page 10; Adam Hart-Davis:
    page 21 (top)
Shutterstock: Suzanne Tucker: page 5 (top); Tomasz Trojanowski:
    page 13 (bottom); Anthony Hall: backgrounds, page 15 (top);
    Anatoly Tiplyashin: page 16; Andreas Guskos: page 17 (center right);
    Martin Rose: pages 18–19; Saveliev Alexey Alexsandrovich: page 19;
    Maxim Petrichuk: page 24; Peter Weber: front cover
Zipp Speed Weaponry: page 17 (left)

Illustrations:
Mark Walker: page 6

Every effort has been made to trace the owners of copyrighted material.

Library and Archives Canada Cataloguing in Publication

Bow, James, 1972-
    Cycling science / James Bow.

(Sports science)
Includes index.
ISBN 978-0-7787-4535-8 (bound).--ISBN 978-0-7787-4552-5 (pbk.)

    1. Cycling--Juvenile literature. 2. Sports sciences--Juvenile
literature. I. Title. II. Series: Sports science (St. Catharines, Ont.)

GV1043.5.B69 2008   j796.601'5   C2008-907025-9

Library of Congress Cataloging-in-Publication Data

Bow, James.
    Cycling science / James Bow.
        p. cm. -- (Sports science)
    Includes index.
    ISBN 978-0-7787-4552-5 (pbk. : alk. paper) -- ISBN 978-0-7787-4535-8
(pbk. : alk. paper)
    1. Cycling--Juvenile literature. 2. Sports Sciences--Juvenile literature.
I. Title. II. Series.

GV1043.5.B69 2008
796.6--dc22

                                                          2008046275

Crabtree Publishing Company

www.crabtreebooks.com   1-800-387-7650

Published in Canada
Crabtree Publishing
616 Welland Ave.
St. Catharines, Ontario
L2M 5V6

Published in the United States
Crabtree Publishing
PMB16A
350 Fifth Ave., Suite 3308
New York, NY 10118

Published in 2009 by CRABTREE PUBLISHING COMPANY.
All rights reserved. No part of this publication may be reproduced,
stored in a retrieval system or be transmitted in any form or by
any means, electronic, mechanical, photocopying, recording, or
otherwise, without the prior written permission of Crabtree
Publishing Company. In Canada: We acknowledge the financial
support of the Government of Canada through the Book Publishing
Industry Development Program (BPIDP) for our publishing
activities. © 2009 The Brown Reference Group plc.

Contents

Introducing Cycling

The invention of the bicycle gave people the freedom to move around with speed and little cost. As cycling technology has advanced, so too has the speed and skill of the people who compete in the different types of **cyclosport**.

From BMX and cyclocross to mountain biking and road racing, competitive cyclosport demands a remarkable level of fitness and skill from the rider and reliability and outstanding performance from the bike.

The CSC pro cycling team compete in the team time-trial stage of the Tour de France.

Cycle science

Bicycles have come a long way since Baron von Drais invented his "running machine" in 1817 (see pages 18–19).

NEW WORDS

Cyclosport: Any sport that involves using bicycles, such as BMX, mountain biking, or road racing.

Modern bikes are amazing machines made from the latest materials. They rely on basic scientific principles. Simple gears allow riders to scale even the steepest mountain peaks and race down the other side at breathtaking speeds. And if the bike has come a long way, think about the human machine that propels it along at such an incredible rate. Coaches are turning to science to come up with the best training plan to get the most from the riders. Cyclists are now jumping higher, racing faster, and performing amazing tricks.

⬆ *BMX riders perform stunts that seem to defy the laws of physics.*

LOOK CLOSER

Try a triathlon

Not content with cycling? Why not try a **triathlon**? On a standard course, triathletes swim about one mile (1.5 km), cycle 25 miles (40 km), and then finish with a six mile (ten km) run. The ultimate fitness test is the Ironman triathlon, during which the triathletes swim 2.5 miles (3.8 km), cycle 112 miles (180 km), and end with a 26-mile (42.2-km) marathon.

Triathlon: A sport in which competitors swim, run, and cycle in consecutive legs.

Muscle Power

If the bicycle is a racecar, then the body is the engine. Muscles in the legs provide the power to push down on the pedals, which moves the bike forward.

The muscles consist of tiny fibers that **contract** and relax to move the bones. In cycling, muscles called the quadriceps and hamstrings attached to the thighbone work with the gastrocnemius and soleus attached to the shinbone. These muscles contract and relax in sequence to move the legs and push the pedals.

Powerful muscles in the legs push the pedals to drive the bike forward.

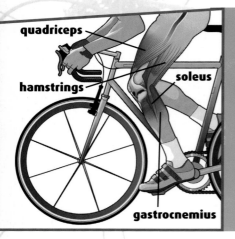

quadriceps

hamstrings

soleus

gastrocnemius

LOOK CLOSER

Muscle levers

Bones are levers that pivot around the joints. When muscles contract, they provide the pulling force to move the bones closer together. The bones swing at the joints, allowing the arms and legs to bend. When the muscles relax, the bones move back into place.

NEW WORDS

Contract: When the fibers in the muscles shrink to draw the bones together.

Muscles work in pairs. The quadriceps contract to push one leg down on one pedal. The hamstrings in the same leg relax. At the same time, the hamstrings in the other leg contract on the upstroke of the other pedal. The quadriceps in the same leg relax.

Muscle fibers

There are two types of muscle fibers. Fast-twitch fibers work quickly but they also tire quickly. They provide bursts of speed, such as a sprint to the finish line. Slow-twitch fibers work much more slowly, but they can carry on working at the same rate for much longer. They provide the **endurance** for longer races.

Bundles of tiny fibers make up the muscles that move the legs.

FACT!

▶▶▶▶▶▶▶▶▶

Pedal power

Each rider continuously generates an average 220 watts of power during a stage of the Tour de France. That's enough power to light 22 low-energy lightbulbs!

Endurance: The ability of an athlete to exercise for long periods of time.

Food for Fuel

A competitive cyclist needs to eat the right balance of nutrients to ensure the body has enough energy to get through the race.

Carbohydrates are sugars. Sugar is energy for the body. Simple carbohydrates can be found in many fruits and refined grains, such as white rice. Complex carbohydrates are found in many vegetables and whole grains, such as brown rice. Complex carbohydrates take longer to break down in the body, so they provide a slow-release source of energy.

Cyclists also need a lot of protein in their food. Protein builds and repairs the body's tissues and muscles. Cereal grains, meat, and dairy products are sources of protein.

The perfect food

An energy bar packs nutrients into a convenient and portable snack. But a banana is a better snack. Bananas are full of carbohydrates, vitamins, and potassium, and they are easy to digest. Better still, the banana's "packaging" is biodegradable.

Fats are another source of energy. The body uses these vital **nutrients** to build cells, especially in the brain and nerve tissue. Fats also help the body process certain vitamins. But not all fats are good for the body. Some, called saturated fats, are unhealthy because they clog blood vessels and may cause heart disease. Foods such as fish, nuts, and vegetable oils are rich in healthy unsaturated fats.

Trace nutrients

The body also needs traces of vitamins and minerals to work properly. These vital nutrients support body processes such as growth and repair. They also help the body fight disease. They are found in a wide range of foods.

LOOK CLOSER

Take a drink

All the energy from food would be useless without the water in the body fluids that transport it to the muscles. Cyclists also release water through sweat. Sweat cools the body when it evaporates. A full water bottle is vital during any race.

People need to eat a balanced variety of foods (shown in this food pyramid) to stay healthy.

►►►►►►►► Sweaty sport

FACT!

Cyclists lose 0.2 gallons (0.8 liters) of sweat per hour during a stage of the Tour de France. For the 141 cyclists who finished the 2007 race, that adds up to enough sweat to fill about 150 bathtubs.

Training for Success

All cyclists follow a strict program of exercise and rest to build muscles and prepare their bodies for a major race.

Intense exercise damages muscles. The body releases chemicals called cytokines, which increase the flow of blood and other fluids to the muscles, making them sore and swollen. Professional cyclists train hard to push their muscles to the limits and then train less so that the body can recover. Massages help soothe sore muscles, but nothing works better than sleep. Muscles use this downtime to repair and grow stronger.

Training targets

Personal trainers help to build a program for each cyclist to follow. In **aerobic conditioning**, bikers use a heart-rate monitor or a power meter

◄ *A cyclist tests how efficiently her body uses oxygen in a sports science laboratory.*

NEW WORDS ● ● ● ● ● ● ● ● ● ● ● ● ● ● ● ● ● ● ●

Aerobic conditioning: Exercising to improve the way in which the body uses oxygen.

LOOK CLOSER

Cycle computers

Many cyclists use computers mounted on the handlebars to chart their performance. Sensors on the bike measure things such as speed and cadence (the rate at which the pedals turn) and calculate power output. Sensors on the rider can measure things such as heart rate and **calories** burned.

to stay in their "aerobic training zone," keeping a high but steady heart rate during prolonged exercise. Cyclists keep training logs to record the dates of training rides, distances traveled, average speeds, heart rate, and much more. From this, the cyclist can chart his or her progress and figure out what needs more work.

FACT!

▶ ▶ ▶ ▶ ▶ ▶ ▶ ▶

Hearty cyclist

At rest, Lance Armstrong's huge heart beats about 32 times every minute (compared to the average 72 beats per minute), pumping twice as much blood around the body than an average person.

Cycling and drugs

Races are supposed to be won by cyclists who ride to the limit of their natural ability. Some cyclists turn to performance-enhancing drugs to gain an advantage. Many drugs have valid medical uses, but they are for fixing problems, not cheating in races.

➡ *American cyclist Lance Armstrong is the sixtime winner of the Tour de France.*

Calories: A measure of the amount of energy provided by food or the energy used during exercise.

The Bicycle

Since bikes were invented in 1817, manufacturers have added gears for more power, used lighter materials such as carbon in place of steel, and developed tires for grip and a smooth ride.

In 2000, the most expensive bikes cost around $2,000. Today, pro cyclists ride bikes that sell for $20,000. The price increase is the result of using high-tech materials, such as **carbon fiber**, to make the forks and frames. Computers refine and specialize the bike designs.

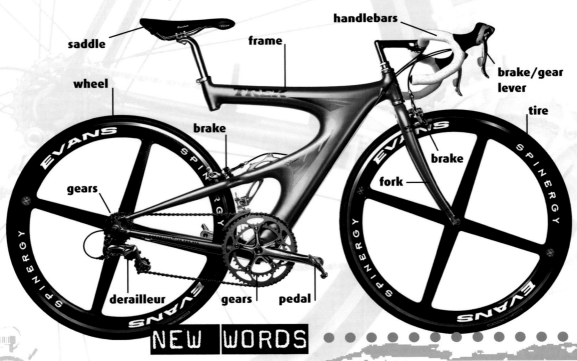

saddle · frame · handlebars · brake/gear lever · wheel · tire · brake · gears · brake · fork · derailleur · gears · pedal

NEW WORDS

Carbon fiber: A strong, lightweight material made by gluing together thin strands of carbon.

LOOK CLOSER

"Old Faithful"

In 1993, Scottish cyclist Graeme Obree and his bike, "Old Faithful," rode 32.06 miles (51.596 kilometers) in one hour, breaking the world hour record. He broke the record again in 1994. Obree built his own bike in an unusual design. Crouched in his seat, his arms were folded by his side and his legs kept a narrow profile.

Different types of bikes

Cyclosport ranges from road races, where bikes are built for speed, to off-road races, where a rugged frame is vital. On a recumbent, the rider sits as if in an easy chair, leaning back over the rear wheel. A low center of gravity keeps the rider stable and makes the bike more **aerodynamic**. These bikes hold most of the speed records, but were banned from races in 1934.

People who use bikes to get to and from school need a design that balances these extremes. If you need a bike but lack space, folding bikes fold down into a compact shape when not in use.

Bicycle History

1817 Baron von Drais invents a "running machine" with two wheels and the ability to steer, but no pedals.

1817

1845 Pneumatic tire invented.

1864 Pedal-driven bike invented.

1870 First use of wire-spoked wheel.

1876 Early caliper brake patented.

1886 Steel tube frame cuts weight, not strength.

1896 First three-speed gear patented.

1933 Rugged "streamlined" bikes become favorites with American teens for next 40 years.

1933

1970 Bicycle motocross (BMX) sparked by movie *On Any Sunday*.

1975 First carbon-fiber frames appear.

1987 First modern aerobars.

1994 First mass-produced hydraulic disk brakes.

Aerodynamic: Having a streamlined shape that reduces drag when moving through the air.

Frame and Forks

A bike needs a lightweight but sturdy frame to support the rider's weight. **Composite materials** and a strong diamond frame design help in this challenge.

The first frames were made of steel, which is strong but heavy. Aluminum is lighter than steel but not as strong. Titanium is stronger than aluminum but not as light. Eventually, frame builders came across a material with all the desired properties. Carbon fiber is strong but light. It is made from threads of carbon, which gives it a "grain." This results in more strength but only in one direction. Carbon-fiber frames do not last as long as those made from traditional metals, but the material holds great promise.

Saddle, bars, and forks

The saddle needs to be comfortable. It must also be angled so that the rider can put the full force of the legs against the pedals.

Suspension forks give a smooth ride over rough ground.

NEW WORDS

Composite materials: Combinations of materials developed by scientists to have special properties.

A typical frame consists of two triangles joined to form a diamond running between the handlebars and the rear wheel.

top tube

top stay

seat tube

fork tube

steering fork

down tube

chain stay

The handlebars allow the rider to turn the front wheel and steer, but also to rest the arms and hold the upper body steady, providing a strong base from which to work the legs.

Suspension forks make riding over rough ground more comfortable. These forks also make the bike easier to steer by keeping the wheels on the ground longer for greater **traction**.

LOOK CLOSER

Superbike

British cyclist Chris Boardman won the gold medal in the 1992 Olympic games. He rode a revolutionary carbon-fiber "superbike" made by Lotus Engineering and designed by Mike Burrows.

Traction: The gripping force between the bicycle's wheels and the ground.

Wheels and Tires

Without wheels, bicycles would be useless. Pedals transfer the force of the rider's legs to the wheel hubs, and the spokes transfer the force to each wheel. The force moves from the wheels to the ground.

Gyroscopic action keeps a bicycle upright when it is moving. The **inertia** of the spinning wheels makes it hard to change their direction or the angle of spin. The faster a cyclist rides, the more stable the bicycle. The enemy of all this power is friction. Anything that rubs against anything has to overcome this **drag**. Compare dragging a bicycle sideways to rolling it forward to feel the force of friction.

Tires

The air-filled tires smooth out the ride. The rubber and the air absorb shocks and make the ride more comfortable. Road racers favor thin tires to reduce wind resistance, while mountain bikes and BMX riders use fat, grooved tires to grip rough ground.

➡ *The spokes give the wheel its strength.*

NEW WORDS

Inertia: The property of a moving object that causes it to carry on moving.

LOOK CLOSER

Disk wheels

Spokes are light, but they catch the wind as the rider picks up speed. Disk wheels have smoother surfaces, allowing the bike to cut through the air. While disk wheels cut down on wind resistance, they catch wind blowing from the side, which makes steering more difficult.

Tubular tires are tubes of rubber that are glued onto the wheel. Clinchers have a U-shaped cross-section and a "bead" (hoop of steel wire) that holds the tire onto the wheel rim. Tubular tires can be filled with more air and there is less chance of a puncture. Clinchers are cheaper, easier to repair, and their rigid structure makes for a faster ride.

Repairing a puncture

Cyclists need a puncture kit and pump to fix punctures on the road. This will close a hole long enough to get home, where permanent repairs can be made.

Brief History of Wheels and Tires

3500 BCE First known use of a wheel (a potter's wheel in Mesopotamia).

3200 BCE Wheels used on Mesopotamian chariots.

2000 BCE Spokes invented by the Egyptians.

1400 BCE Wheels appear in Europe.

100 BCE–500 CE Romans make extensive use of wheels for chariots, carriages, and coaches.

100 BCE–500 CE

1802 Invention of the tension spoke.

1844 Charles Goodyear invents vulcanized rubber, later used to make tires.

1844

1888 John Dunlop invents the pneumatic (air-filled) tire for the bicycle.

NEW WORDS

Inertia: The property of a moving object that causes it to carry on moving.

Gears and Transmission

Pedals transmit muscle power directly to drive the wheel, which is fine on level ground but tiring when climbing uphill. This is where gears help.

Gears change the amount the bike moves forward with each turn of the pedals. The gears at the front of the **transmission** are called chainwheels. A strong metal chain links the chainwheels to gears called sprockets on the rear wheel. Spring-loaded derailleurs move the chain between the different gears. The front derailleur moves the chain between the chainwheels, and the rear derailleur moves the chain between the sprockets.

Changing gear

On most bikes, the rider changes gear by shifting gear levers mounted on the handlebars. A cable links the gear lever to the spring in the derailleur. Pressing or twisting the gear shifter changes the **tension** in the cable, moving the derailleur and chain over the range of gears.

NEW WORDS

Tension: The force that pulls on a wire or string, keeping it taut.

Cyclists use a low gear (small chainwheel and large sprocket) to ride up steep hills. Pedaling is easier, but the bicycle moves more slowly. On level ground, a high gear (large chainwheel and small sprocket) makes pedaling slower but the bike moves faster.

Freewheeling

The freewheel lets the wheels spin faster than the gears would otherwise allow. The bike can then coast, giving the cyclist a well-deserved rest.

Mountain bikes need a wide range of gears to cope with steep hills.

The rear derailleur moves the chain between sprockets.

LOOK CLOSER

Gear ratios

A 2:1 gear ratio means that one gear is twice the size of the gear it turns. A 3:1 gear ratio spins the wheels three times for every one turn of the pedals. The bike will go slower, but it puts more power into the wheel, pushing both the cyclist and the bike uphill more easily.

Transmission: The system of cables, chain, and gears that transmits power from the pedals to the wheel.

Slowing Down

Since the wheels make the bike move forward, the wheels must also stop turning to make the bike stop.

Most bicycles use one of two brake systems. Rim brakes use brake pads to push against the side of the rims to stop the bike. In disk brakes, the brake pads push against a disk connected to the wheel axle.

Caliper brakes are rim brakes. They have two arms that cross at a pivot above the wheel. Levers on the handlebars allow the rider to apply rim brakes through a tension wire. Squeezing the levers moves the arms together, pinching the wheel rim between them.

Since they work well in wet, muddy conditions, many mountain bikes use disk brakes.

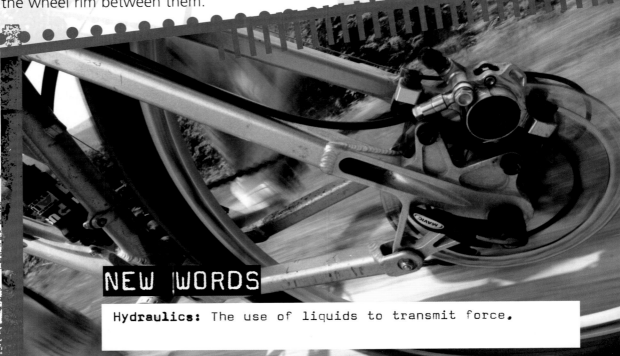

NEW WORDS

Hydraulics: The use of liquids to transmit force.

Fixed wheel

Bikes with fixed wheels do not have brakes. They have a sprocket screwed directly to the hub, so the bike cannot freewheel and the rider cannot coast. The rider resists the turning of the pedals to stop the bike. Track bikes are usually fixed wheels, but many commuters and couriers use fixed-wheel bikes in cities. Fixed-wheel bikes are light and easy to maintain, but they can be hard when climbing hills. Cyclists must also pedal very rapidly as they descend.

Caliper brakes push against the rim to stop the bike.

Some mountain-bike wheels are too wide for calipers. The distance between the pivot and brake pad is long enough for the arm to flex, which costs precious braking power. Cantilever brakes solve this problem by having separate **pivot** points to bring each arm's full pressure to bear on the wheel rims.

Disk brakes

Disk brakes use **hydraulics** to stop the bike. Liquids do not compress easily and so they are very good at transferring force. The hydraulic fluid flows through a hose to push the pistons on the disk caliper. The caliper then pushes the brake pads against the disk on the wheel to stop the bike. Disk brakes work well in poor conditions, and they do not wear out the wheel rims.

LOOK CLOSER

Coaster brakes

Coaster brakes are called back-pedal brakes because pedaling backward works a drum brake in the rear wheel to stop the bike. Since these brakes only work on the rear wheel, they do not stop a bike as well as rim or disk brakes that work on both wheels.

Pivot: A stationary point around which a rotation takes place.

Cutting Through the Air

 t is not only the bike that is built with aerodynamics in mind. All the cyclist's gear is designed to slice through the air with minimum effort.

The helmet and gear of Olympic road-race champion Nicole Cooke help her slice through the air.

Look at any professional on the track or during the time-trial stage of a major race. The riders use a range of aerodynamic gear to help their bodies cut through the air.

FACT!

▶ ▶ ▶ ▶ ▶ ▶ ▶ ▶ ▶

Speedy helmet

Over 15.5 miles (25 kilometers), an aero helmet can give a pro cyclist a 16-second advantage over an opponent. It may not sound like much, but seconds can help to win races.

Aero helmet

Most cycling helmets are round to fit the shape of the head. The front of an aero helmet is like a regular helmet, but it narrows into a long point at the back of the head. The aero helmet may look rather strange, but it helps smooth out the wind flow around the head. Cutting down wind resistance can save valuable seconds in a race.

Italian professional sprinter Mario Cippolini was famous for his custom-made skin suits.

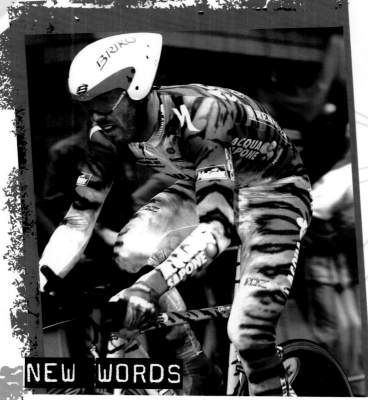

LOOK CLOSER

Windy tunnels

Pro cyclists test their gear and bikes in purpose-built wind tunnels. Scientists record the air flow around the cyclists as they ride on a static machine. The tests highlight poor air flow, which results in drag and slows the cyclist down. Wind-tunnel tests also help cyclists ride with the best body position.

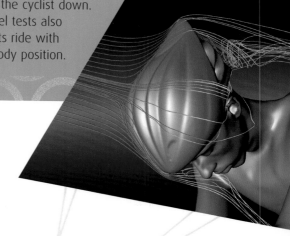

Suits and shoes

Many cyclists wear body suits that fit the shape of their bodies and improve the air flow around them. A cyclist's feet are moving all the time, so road racers often wear overshoes on top of their cycling shoes to cut through the air with minimum **drag**. All these features save time. In a close race, a few milliseconds separate winners from losers.

NEW WORDS

Drag: The force that resists the movement of an object through the air.

Cycle Skills

For short sprints on the track and steep ascents on a mountain stage of the Tour de France, cyclists need balance, coordination, and skill to win the race.

A cyclist leans back over the rear wheel to descend a steep hill.

On the straight, a cyclist pumps his or her legs to overcome the force of **friction**. The cyclist also crouches over the handlebars to make his or her body as small as possible. This cuts down on the drag caused by wind resistance.

Up and down

Cyclists fight **gravity** climbing hills. They stand and put their weight on the pedals to get more power. Gravity helps cyclists down hills. Coasting speeds may be 45 miles (72 kilometers) an hour, so the riders tuck in and let gravity do its job. Only friction and drag slow them down.

NEW WORDS

Friction: The force that opposes movement over a surface.

24

LOOK CLOSER

Pedal power

With normal pedals, the cyclists can only apply force on the downstroke. The recovery phase begins when the pedal reaches the bottom. The cyclist's leg muscles then relax as the pedal rises. Clipless pedals use a special shoe that locks into each pedal. Clipping the shoes to the pedals adds power to the upstroke.

Sprints

Sprinting calls upon an enormous effort from tired leg muscles to make a dash for the finish line. First, the sprinter tucks in behind another rider. The leading rider does all the work and shields the sprinter from the wind. The sprinter then uses high gears to ensure that all the muscle power transforms into a sudden burst of acceleration.

Cyclists lean into corners to make tight turns.

LOOK CLOSER

Countersteering

Cyclists lean into curves. Tilting the bike moves it in the direction the cyclist wants to go. But gyroscopic action makes it hard to tilt a bike when it is moving forward. The cyclist turns the wheel to disrupt the balance of the bicycle. By pulling the wheel to the left, the bike leans right. By leaning right, the bike turns right. This is called countersteering.

Gravity: The force of attraction between objects due to their mass.

Different Disciplines

There are many different types of cyclosport, from the acrobatic feats of bicycle motocross (BMX) and mountain biking to the bursts of acceleration on the track and the long-distance challenge of road racing.

In road racing, the cyclists set off in a group and race along the open road to the finish line. Teams of cyclists ride in pacelines to take advantage of **slipstreaming**, in which riders at the front reduce the wind resistance on the riders behind.

BMX racing

Bicycle motocross (BMX) races are on dirt tracks, with jumps, mud traps, and banked corners, among other obstacles. Races usually last just 30 to 40 seconds. BMX riders often perform acrobatic tricks such as backflips.

FACT!

▶ ▶ ▶ ▶ ▶ ▶ ▶ ▶

Tour de France

The 2007 Tour de France was 2,217 miles (3,568 kilometers) long. The average speed of the winner, Spanish cyclist Alberto Contador, was 24.5 miles (39.43 kilometers) per hour.

NEW WORDS

Slipstreaming: When a cyclist tucks in behind another rider to save energy by cutting down on drag.

26

These tricks were first done on the dirt track. As they became more popular, ramps, called funboxes, and pipes were built for freestyle competitions.

Off-road cycling

Mountain biking races can be cross-country, downhill, uphill, or slalom. In all these races, the riders push their bikes through punishing terrain.

In slalom, a cyclist must move his or her bike around a series of gates like an alpine skier. Mountain bikers must repair their own bikes during a race, but cyclocross racers can use up to three machines, switching when their bikes get too clogged with dirt. They push their bikes up short, steep hills and cycle along muddy paths through woodland trails.

On the track

Track cyclists take the race indoors on a purpose-built **velodrome** with banked curves. These allow the cyclists to corner at top speed. Starting gates hold back cyclists until the race begins. Bikes are fixed gear, so riders must keep turning the pedals until the race is over.

A mountain biker lands a backflip over a huge jump.

Velodrome: A purpose-built indoor arena for bike racing. Modern velodromes have steeply banked oval tracks.

The Future of Cycling

As the cost of fuel increases, it might be the everyday cyclist who pushes his or her bike to highway speeds—not in a race but on the way to work.

Space-age materials have revolutionized cyclosport, with carbon fibers being used to build lighter and stronger frames, forks, and other components. Eventually, **carbon nanotubes** may offer even stronger material. New, flexible, lightweight materials could even replace the puncture-prone air-filled tire.

LOOK CLOSER

Human-powered vehicles

Human-powered vehicles may soon bring commuters to work without polluting the air. These new vehicles will be faster than normal bikes and feature an outer shell for protection. Futurists are already calling for bicycle expressways, with enclosed lanes to protect against the elements and pumped air to ensure the wind is always blowing from behind.

NEW WORDS

Carbon nanotubes: Sheets of carbon atoms arranged in the form of tubes.

Cycling changes

Computers are getting smaller, so it is inevitable that more of them will end up on bikes, monitoring speed, power, and heart rate and relaying the data to the cyclist or trainer in the pace car behind.

Canadian Sam Whittingham set a land-speed record of 81.25 miles (130 km) per hour in a recumbent.

Harald Cramer's futuristic ORYX is a time-trial bike made with aerodynamics in mind.

Cyclists will also change. Doctors will find ways to improve training programs and nutrition plans. Some cyclists will find new ways to cheat the system by using new drugs. Some international officials have suggested using devices to monitor cyclists 24 hours a day.

The basic principle of the bicycle has changed little since the **penny farthing**. But it is impossible to imagine today's riders winning races on those early bikes. Cyclosport has changed dramatically in the last 50 years. We can only imagine what it will be like in the next 50 years.

Penny farthing: A popular 19th century bicycle, with the front wheel far larger than the rear wheel.

Glossary

Aerobic conditioning: Exercising to improve the way in which the body uses oxygen.

Aerodynamic: Having a streamlined shape that reduces drag when moving through the air.

Calories: A measure of the amount of energy provided by food or the energy used during exercise.

Carbon fiber: A strong, lightweight material made by gluing together thin strands of carbon.

Carbon nanotubes: Sheets of carbon atoms arranged in the form of tubes.

Composite materials: Combinations of materials developed by scientists to have special properties.

Contract: When the fibers in the muscles shrink to draw the bones together.

Cyclosport: Any sport that involves using bicycles, such as BMX, mountain biking, or road racing.

Drag: The force that resists the movement of an object through the air.

Endurance: The ability of an athlete to exercise for long periods of time.

Friction: The force that opposes movement over a surface.

Gravity: The force of attraction between objects due to their mass.

Hydraulics: The use of liquids to transmit force.

Inertia: The property of a moving object that causes it to carry on moving.

Nutrients: Substances such as carbohydrates and vitmins that the body needs to work properly.

Penny farthing: A popular 19th century bicycle, with the front wheel far larger than the rear wheel.

Pivot: A stationary point around which a rotation takes place.

Slipstreaming: When a cyclist tucks in behind another rider to save energy by cutting down on drag.

Tension: The force that pulls on a wire or string, keeping it taut.

Traction: The gripping force between the bicycle's wheels and the ground.

Transmission: The system of cables, chain, and gears that transmits power from the pedals to the wheel.

Triathlon: A sport in which competitors swim, run, and cycle in consecutive legs.

Velodrome: A purpose-built indoor arena for bike racing. Modern velodromes have steeply banked oval tracks.

Find Out More

Books

Crossingham, John, and Bonna Rouse. *Cycling in Action (Sports in Action)*. New York: Crabtree Publishing Company, 2002.

Fridell, Ron. *Sports Technology (Cool Science)*. Minneapolis, Minnesota: Lerner Publications, 2008.

Gardner, Robert. *Bicycle Science Projects: Physics on Wheels (Science Fair Success)*. Berkeley Heights, New Jersey: Enslow Publishers, 2004.

Graham, Ian. *The Science of a Bicycle (The Science of)*. Milwaukee, Wisconsin: Gareth Stevens Publishing, 2009.

Pinchuk, Amy. *Best Book of Bikes, The (Popular Mechanics for Kids)*. Toronto, Ontario: Maple Tree Press, 2003.

Web sites

The official website of USA Cycling includes useful information about the different forms of cyclosport.

www.usacycling.org

The Exploratorium website includes video clips and animations that explain the science behind the bicycle and the sport of cycling.

www.exploratorium.edu/cycling/

The How Stuff Works website includes an extremely informative article that explains the science and technology behind the bicycle.

www.howstuffworks.com/bicycle.htm

Index

32